Disney's
Flubber

A novel by Cathy East Dubowski
Based on the motion picture from Walt Disney Pictures
Screenplay by John Hughes and Bill Walsh
Produced by John Hughes and Ricardo Mestres
Directed by Les Mayfield

DISNEY
PRESS

NEW YORK

First Edition
1 3 5 7 9 10 8 6 4 2

Library of Congress Catalog Card Number: 97-80050
ISBN: 0-7868-4136-2

CHAPTER ONE

The sun rose on a cheerful yellow house surrounded by a white picket fence.

But the house's paint was peeling. A few pickets in the fence had fallen out like missing teeth. In the front yard the overgrown grass had taken a rusty lawn mower prisoner.

The backyard was even worse. It looked more like a junkyard with machine parts and bits and pieces of electronics littering the ground.

In the middle of the mess, a garbage can stood on a small homemade launchpad.

Riiiiiiiiiing!

Upstairs, in the second-floor bedroom, an old-fashioned metal alarm clock rang. A big lump on the bed stirred. Then a man's hand shot out from beneath the tangled covers.

Riiiiiiiiiing!

He felt across the jumble of junk on the nightstand. Past the books, the reading glasses, pencils, and calculators. Past a framed photo of a pretty, smiling woman with short brown hair.

Riiiiiiiiiing!

The vibrating alarm clock skittered across the nightstand and tumbled off the edge.

Riiiiii—thunk! It landed upside down—on the Off button. The alarm finally stopped ringing.

The man's hand slammed down on a small metal detonator attached to a plunger.

Booom!

The garbage can on the backyard launchpad exploded into the sky!

"HONEY!" called a pleasant woman's voice from downstairs. "ARE YOU UP?"

Professor Phillip Brainard dug himself out of the tangled covers. With a yawn, he swung his feet over the side of the bed and felt along the cluttered floor for his slippers. One foot slipped into a Kleenex box. The other squirmed into an old heating pad cover. "Up and ready for a new day!" he shouted.

"OH, WHAT A BEAUTIFUL MORNING!" the woman's voice sang out.

"Oh, what a beautiful day!" the professor sang back. He stood up and reached for his bathrobe.

But instead, he yanked a flowery slipcover off a chair and threw that around his shoulders. Then he headed downstairs, absently stepping around piles of books, file folders, cups, mail, and laundry.

Seconds later—*Clunk!*—the garbage can landed right side up by the front curb just as the front door opened.

The professor stepped out onto the front porch to fetch his paper, wearing a flowered slipcover for a robe and tissue box-heating pad slippers.

Across the street two sanitation workers stopped in midtoss.

The professor waved as he clunked down the driveway to pick up his paper. "Morning, boys!" he said with a cheery smile.

The younger worker stared at him. Was this guy crazy or what?

"He's a professor," the older worker explained. "Science."

"Oh." The young guy nodded. *That* explained it!

But the professor's smile melted as he read the morning's headline: COLLEGE FLUNKS MATH! FINANCIER SET TO FORECLOSE ON MEDFIELD COLLEGE.

CHAPTER TWO

The professor yanked open his paper. He wandered into his neighbors' front yard as he read the rest of the bad news.

One photo showed the president of Medfield College, Dr. Sara Jean Reynolds, the same pretty brunette woman in the photo on the professor's nightstand.

Another photo showed a sour-looking man in his sixties. He was financier Chester Hoenicker, the man who was threatening to shut down the school because they couldn't pay back money he had loaned them.

This is terrible! Professor Brainard thought as he walked up the wrong steps onto his neighbors' front porch.

I love teaching at Medfield! he thought as he opened the front door and walked into his neighbors' house.

4

I've got to do something—fast! he thought as he walked down the hall and sat down at his neighbors' breakfast table.

His neighbors—a young man, his wife, their toddler, and a little baby in a high chair—stared at him.

"How can you replace a college with an industrial park?" he demanded. "It's an outrage—"

The professor looked up. Puzzled, he stared at the baby.

The baby shook his head and pointed with his spoon to the back door. Professor Brainard smiled sheepishly and stood up. "Once again, my apologies."

The family went back to eating their breakfast. They were used to their crazy, absentminded neighbor.

Back in his own home, the professor dressed quickly and hurried downstairs. *Mmm-mmm!* He could smell fresh coffee and a home-cooked breakfast sizzling on the stove.

"BREAKFAST IS READY!" the woman's voice called out. "HURRY UP!"

The professor stopped in the entry hall to adjust his tie in the mirror. A puzzled look crossed his face. Then he chuckled. His face was coated with shaving cream! "Forgot to shave!"

He patted his pockets till he found his razor. Turning back to the mirror, he yanked some flowers out of their vase. He swizzled his razor in the flower water. Then he quickly shaved.

Soon he sat down and smiled across the breakfast table (the correct one this time). "Good morning, Weebo."

Weebo hovered four feet off the ground.

Her "eye"—which was really a six-inch color video screen—blinked.

On that screen was a housewife from an old commercial smiling from a dream kitchen saying: "NOTHING GETS MY FAMILY OFF TO A GOOD START IN THE MORNING LIKE A HEARTY, WHOLESOME BREAKFAST."

Weebo wasn't a woman.

She wasn't the professor's wife.

She was a computer. A computer that flew. And she was one of Phillip Brainard's most wonderful inventions.

Weebo was a shiny black magnesium oval about twelve inches wide. She could fly, hover, somersault, and land using four powerful microthrusters. In the center of her "face" a telescoping video camera lens stuck out like a nose. She also had a Polaroid camera.

She was part computer. Part housekeeper. Part secretary. The absentminded professor couldn't get along without her.

Weebo could talk, too—just like a human woman.

"DID YOU SEE THE PAPER THIS MORN-ING?" Weebo's screen flipped up and displayed an image of the paper the professor had been reading.

The family robot, Webber, another of the professor's inventions, swung around and poured creamer in his coffee.

The professor scowled. "If I could figure out this metastable compounds business, I could save the school. A new energy source would be worth a fortune!"

"BETTER HURRY UP," Weebo said. "THE LOAN IS DUE AT THE END OF THE SCHOOL YEAR."

"I think I'm getting close. Not to worry," Professor Brainard replied. He gulped some coffee. "Can I see my schedule for today, please?"

Weebo's screen flipped up. Slowly, one by one, the professor's scheduled appointments for the day scrolled up on the screen.

There were his regular morning classes. Lunch. A faculty meeting. Then more classes till 4 P.M.

Professor Brainard leaned back, puzzled. "Nothing after class?"

Weebo said nothing.

The professor folded his arms. He had a really strong feeling that there was something . . . something *important* he was supposed to do today. But what? He rubbed his chin and stared at the floor.

Weebo's screen scrolled up, revealing one more appointment:

6:30 P.M.: MARRIAGE TO DR. SARA JEAN REYNOLDS.

Professor Brainard looked up . . . two and a half seconds *after* Weebo slammed her screen shut.

Professor Brainard grinned and guessed, "Haircut, right?"

Weebo just bobbed in the air and again said nothing.

A few minutes later Professor Brainard bustled out the back door into the bright sunshine, carrying his hat, his briefcase, lunch in a paper sack, and a raincoat. "Have a nice day, Weebo. Call me if anything comes up!"

Weebo hovered near the screen door, watching him go.

And then her eyelike screen slowly opened—filled with throbbing cartoon hearts.

Every wire, every circuit, every nut and bolt in her being ached.

Poor Weebo.

The little computer was in love with the professor!

CHAPTER THREE

Professor Brainard hurried across the beautiful tree-lined Medfield College campus. He glanced at his watch. Three-thirty! How did it get so late?

He dashed into an ivy-covered building and into the room where he taught his afternoon class.

But the professor didn't realize he'd put his watch on upside down. It wasn't three-thirty. It was really only nine o'clock!

"Good morning!" he called out cheerfully. "Or, afternoon, as the case may be."

The roomful of art students sitting in front of their easels stared in confusion, their pencils in midair. What was Professor Phillip Brainard, the chemistry professor, doing in an *art* class?

Professor Brainard grabbed an orange from the bowl of fruit the students had painted the day before. "Whoever brought me the orange, the pheasant, and the grapes, thank you." He put down his briefcase. "During our last session we discussed Newton's theory of gravitation. To review . . ." He turned to the blackboard and scribbled a math equation. "Tommy? Would you explain this equation to the class, please? No? Can anyone help Tommy?"

Then the professor noticed something else written on the board. LIFE DRAWING. DR. RICHARDS.

Oops. Wrong class. Blushing, Professor Brainard picked up his briefcase and coat and scooted out the door.

He loved teaching. Now, if he could only find his class . . .

Across campus the president of the university, Dr. Sara Jean Reynolds, stood on her desk.

She was talking on the phone about the college's money problems . . . in a beautiful floor-length white wedding gown.

A tailor fiddled with the hem as Martha George, Sara's plump secretary, beamed in delight.

Sara covered the phone and glanced nervously at her elegant dress. "You don't think it's too much?" she asked her secretary.

"Oh, no!" Martha cried. "It's a wonderful idea to go with the big wedding this time. It does put the pressure on the professor to show up."

Sara crossed her arms. "If he forgets this time, that's it. In his case, once is justifiable. Twice is understandable. But three times—"

She broke off as she noticed handsome Wilson Croft standing in the doorway, a sly smile on his face.

Was he eavesdropping?

Sara hung up the phone. Wilson held up his arms and whisked her down from the desk.

"What are you doing here?" she asked.

"I always come in for your weddings," he said sarcastically.

Martha scowled. She didn't like Wilson Croft one bit. And she didn't like the way he was always chasing after her boss. Sure, he was good-looking and intelligent and successful. But how could you love a guy who was already in love with himself? Shaking her head, Martha ushered the tailor out and closed the door.

Wilson took Sara in his arms, his eyes full of pity. "Why would you put yourself through this again? If Phillip doesn't think enough of you to show up at two weddings, what makes you think he'll show up for a third? Or a fourth?" Wilson shook his head. "I've known Professor Phillip Brainard for years. He loves his work—and *only* his work."

Sara wriggled out of his embrace. "I don't believe that."

"After tonight, you'll know," Wilson said as he left Sara's office. "And I—as always—will be there with my hankie."

Sara wandered over to the window and gazed across her beloved campus. She had to admit she was worried. She held out her hand and gazed at her engagement ring. It was modest, but sweet. Like all engagement rings, a promise.

But it was the *third* one Phillip had given her. Would he keep the promise this time?

CHAPTER FOUR

At lunchtime Sara spotted the professor carrying a greasy paper bag and a stack of notebooks. "Phillip! Over here!"

Professor Brainard hurried over. "What a pleasant surprise!" He smiled at Sara's secretary. "Hi, Judy."

"It's Martha," Martha said automatically for the eighty-seventh time. But she didn't say it in a mean way. Despite his faults, she liked the professor. She thought he was perfect for Sara.

Professor Brainard laid his lunch bag and notebooks on the table and sat down. "I was just going to grade lunch while I ate a few tests. But this is very nice."

Sara smiled affectionately. She was used to the professor's silly mistakes. His brain was so full of brilliant ideas, that ordinary thoughts often got mixed up and squashed into the corners.

"I've been on the phone all morning begging alumni for money," Sara said with a sigh.

"I told you I'm going to come up with something that will make some money for the university," Professor Brainard said.

"Better hurry," Sara said.

"That's what Weebo said," Professor Brainard replied.

Martha shook her head and gushed, "How do you hold it all in?"

The professor looked puzzled. "Like anybody else, Ruthie. I cross my legs real tight."

Martha rolled her eyes. "I'm talking about your excitement."

"Excitement?"

"The wedding!"

"The wedding?"

Martha exchanged a worried glance with Sara.

The professor smacked his head. "Oh, yes, our wedding! Sara and I. I'm looking forward to it. Aren't you, honey?"

"It's today," Sara reminded him.

The professor frowned and took a crumpled soda

can out of his lunch bag. "Today? You're sure?"

"Phillip!"

"It wasn't on my schedule," the professor objected. "I thought I was getting my hair cut. How strange. That's not something Weebo would forget."

Sara shook her head knowingly. She'd seen the way that little computer looked at Phillip. "That's *exactly* what she'd forget."

"Weebo's excited," the professor argued. "You know, she was a little miffed that she couldn't be a bridesmaid." He pulled a half-eaten banana and a rubbery sandwich out of his lunch bag.

"Sweetie, the wedding's today, okay?" Sara said, trying to smile. "Six-thirty. Presbyterian Church on Beech Street. After your last class go home and put on your tuxedo," she suggested. "Then drive to the church and wait."

The professor nodded. "I'll go home, put on the gray suit—"

"Tuxedo!" Martha corrected.

"Tuxedo," he repeated. "And go to the Ethiopian—"

"Presbyterian!" Martha corrected again.

"Got it! Presbyterian Church on . . ."

Martha opened her mouth to tell him, but Sara grabbed her arm to stop her. "Let him get it."

The professor frowned. Why couldn't addresses be as easy to remember as scientific equations? "Eighth Street?" he guessed.

Sara shook her head. "Think of trees."

"Lumber Street?"

"Type of tree."

"Shoe tree."

"It begins with a *B*."

Professor Brainard stared at his fiancée helplessly. He truly couldn't remember.

"Beech Street," she broke down and told him.

"Got it." The professor smiled. "I don't deserve you."

"This is going to be the very last time I try to marry you," she warned. "I love you, but I'm not sure that you can love me."

"That's ridiculous!" he exclaimed. "Of course I love you. I love you with every cell, every molecule, every atom. . . . You know, speaking of atoms, I had the most incredible thought today in an art class I accidentally taught—"

"Prove it to me at six-thirty tonight," Sara interrupted.

"Oh, sure. Of course. Six-thirty. And that's tonight, you say?"

"Tonight." Sara gave the professor a quick kiss.

"Good luck," Martha said with a smile.

The professor opened his mouth to bite his petrified sandwich.

Sara stopped him just in time. "One more thing. It's bad luck to eat garbage on your wedding day."

"Hmm?" The professor gaped at the odd assortment of old, dried-up, half-eaten food on the table before him. His sandwich was coated with fuzzy blue-green mold. "I was wondering what my lunch bag was doing in the wastebasket!"

Drip, drip, drip.

Professor Brainard was doing an experiment in his laboratory. He opened a tiny valve. Yellow liquid flowed through a roller-coaster ride of thin glass tubes and dripped into a small bottle.

Professor Brainard capped the bottle, then

wiped hands on the long lab apron he wore over his teaching clothes.

Excellent, he thought. He slipped the bottle into his briefcase and snapped it shut. Time to go home. Weebo would be expecting him for dinner.

Just then the door opened. "Hello, Phil. Whatcha working on?"

The professor frowned. Wilson Croft. They used to work together. They used to be friends. Not anymore. "Um . . ."

"Can't remember?" Wilson chuckled. "I understand." He strolled over to the lab table to examine the professor's work. "It's a shame your college is shutting down. I read about it in the paper."

"It's not over yet," Professor Brainard said, flipping through a book of notes.

"We're doing fine over at Rutland College," Wilson went on. "No such financial problems." He looked with interest at the professor's notes. "I see you're still looking for your lighter-than-air compound. No luck finding that organic catalyst?"

The professor slammed his notebook closed.

"You don't seem very excited to see me," Wilson said dryly.

"I'm not."

"After all the years we've known each other, studying, working together . . . what happened between us, Phil?"

"I got tired of *you* stealing *my* ideas," the professor said.

Wilson laughed. "And what would you have done with them, Phil? You would have misplaced them. Forgotten them. Lost them. There's no doubt that you're the smarter of the two of us. You have a genius for science. But the science of daily life eludes you."

"I've heard all this before, Wilson."

"I won't deny that I hate you for your brilliance," Wilson went on. "And I am here this weekend to steal your fiancée and make her my wife. What do you say to *that*?"

"You're going to be disappointed," the professor said.

"By the way," Wilson said. "Sara told me the name of the church. But I don't remember. What is it?"

The professor opened his mouth to answer—but couldn't. He thought for a moment. *Trees, trees* . . . "It's on Beech Street!" the professor shouted smugly.

It felt good to slam the door on his way out.

But could he remember the street name long enough to find the church?

CHAPTER FIVE

Bennett Hoenicker slammed on the brakes in front of his father's mansion. He jumped out of his brand-new Jeep, stormed up the steps, and burst through the front door. "Dad!" he bellowed.

Two security guards sitting in the living room exchanged weary looks. Don Wesson put down his auto magazine. Henry Smith turned off the TV.

Bennett Hoenicker, the son of their employer, was handsome, spoiled, and as dumb as dirt. But his father paid them pretty well to keep an eye on him, so they put up with him.

"Where's my father?" Bennett demanded, shoving his way past the two men. Smith and Wesson hurried after the boy as he stomped down the wide hallway, then burst through the library doors.

Chester Hoenicker sat behind a mahogany desk, smoking a cigar and reading the morning newspaper.

"Somebody in your organization screwed up big time!" Bennett shouted. He tossed a sheet of paper onto his father's desk. "I *flunked* chemistry. I'm on academic probation!"

Chester Hoenicker picked up the paper and frowned. Academic probation meant his son couldn't play on the basketball team.

"I'm supposed to get *A*s," Bennett whined. "Or at least that's what I was told."

Mr. Hoenicker glared at his two security guards. "The only reason I loaned this stupid college money was so that *he* could get straight *A*s and go to Harvard Business School." He waved the paper in their faces. "*This* wasn't supposed to happen."

Smith and Wesson gulped nervously.

"We talked to this Professor Brainard guy—the chemistry professor," Smith explained. "But either he didn't understand or he forgot."

"I have a science requirement, you moron," Bennett snapped.

"We could have bought him biology," Smith said to Mr. Hoenicker. "Or geology, or—whatever's the study of bugs."

Bennett snorted. "I can't stand bugs. I hate

animals. And I loathe rocks!"

"And chemicals are better?" Smith asked.

"I thought we'd blow up stuff!" Bennett exclaimed.

"Shut up!" Mr. Hoenicker ordered. "We have to get the F changed to an A."

"It won't work," Bennett said with a pout. "Professor Brainard doesn't live in the real world. He has principles."

Mr. Hoenicker rubbed his hands together, thinking. Then he barked at Smith and Wesson, "Get something on him that we can use to *force* him to change the kid's grade." To his son he added, "When a man says he has principles, it means he can't be bought *cheap*."

CHAPTER SIX

Sara, darling, Professor Brainard thought happily as he tried to tie his tuxedo tie. This time I won't let you down!

"You didn't include the wedding on today's schedule," the professor said to Weebo as he struggled with the tie. "Are you feeling okay?"

But the professor didn't hear her answer. He suddenly stared past her as if he were in a hypnotic trance.

His eyes were glued to the computer on his desk. A complex mathematical formula filled the screen.

"*I* know what I didn't do!" he exclaimed as he sat down at his desk. "I've been bridging the metastable compounds with carbon atoms," he mumbled to himself. "I need to bridge them with an organic *compound*."

His fingers flew across the keyboard, making

the change. "Now it'll work!" he crowed, jumping up from the desk.

"WHAT ABOUT THE WEDDING?" Weebo asked.

But the numbers and formulas spinning in the professor's mind crowded out all other thoughts. He dashed out of the room and down to the chemistry lab in his basement.

The professor tore off his tuxedo jacket and tossed it onto a hook. His mind whirling, he rolled up his sleeves.

Weebo flew downstairs and hovered like a hummingbird in front of the professor's face. "DOES THIS MEAN YOU'VE COME TO YOUR SENSES?"

But the professor didn't answer. His brain nearly exploded with the astonishing light of a brilliant idea.

And there was not one iota of room left in his mind for thoughts of tuxedos, or church names, or wedding bells.

The professor's experiment looked like an elaborate miniature amusement park made of glass beakers, test tubes, torches, and pipes.

Sparkling yellow fluid sizzled as it gushed through the tubes on a wild and crazy ride.

"It's ready," he announced to Weebo.

Quickly the professor opened taps, adjusted the flames of torches, and flipped switches on regulators and meters.

Then his eyes locked onto a batch of sparkling blue fluid bubbling in a mixing tank.

Yellow fluid gurgled into a tap, then spurted into the blue fluid in the tank.

Zap! The tank flashed in a storm of electricity.

The professor plucked a single hair from his tousled mop. "The organic compound," he whispered. He made a wish, as if tossing a coin into a fountain for good luck. Then he dropped the hair into the tank and sealed it shut.

Next he attached two wires. The wires ran to the detonator he'd used that morning to blast the trash to the curb.

He raised the plunger. "A little electrical energy . . ."

Weebo's screen snapped shut.

The professor slammed the plunger.

Blamo!

Flames rocketed up the chimney as the explosion blew out the basement windows of the professor's cheery yellow-and-white house.

In the Presbyterian Church on Beech Street, the organist's fingers ached from playing the same songs over and over and over.

A few of the guests had fallen asleep in the pews.

The minister stared at the tip of his shoe, wondering what his wife had made for dinner.

And the beautiful bride, Sara Jean Reynolds . . . well, she couldn't help herself. A single tear slipped down her cheek and splashed onto a petal of her fading bouquet.

A few rows back in the church pews, Wilson Croft grinned as if he'd just hit a home run. Strike three, Professor Brainless, he thought as he pulled his silk hankie from his pocket. My turn to bat.

CHAPTER SEVEN

"Wow! What a bang!"

Professor Phillip Brainard sat up in his wrecked basement and looked around. His face was covered with black soot. His clothes were torn and singed. Glass crunched underfoot as he walked around, checking the damage.

Most of his equipment was smashed. A worktable was busted in half. The professor glared at the ooze-covered mixing tank. He reared back and gave it an angry kick.

Then he and Weebo headed for the stairs.

Gurgle . . . Sputter . . . Chirp-Chirp-Chirp!

The professor froze. Was that weird sound coming from the mixing tank?

The high-pitched chirping sound grew into a whine . . . as if something *inside* the tank wanted to get *out*!

The tank shuddered, then slowly it rose in the

air. Higher and higher, till it nearly bumped the ceiling.

Suddenly it crashed to the basement floor. The professor stumbled over the debris as he rushed toward the gurgling, moaning tank.

Gooooossssssh! Out oozed a pulsing rubbery green wad of gunk.

The professor leaned closer.

The gunk slithered back into the tank.

Amazed, the professor leaned back on his heels.

And the green goo shyly peeked over the lid of the tank.

The professor leaned to the side. The gunk leaned to the side.

He reached for it, and it reared back.

Wow! the professor thought. Slowly he held up the back of his hand, the way he would try to make friends with a strange dog.

The green gunk reached out and cautiously touched the professor's fingertips—as if testing the temperature, the texture, the scent.

Slowly the professor turned his hand palm up. The strange, rubbery stuff slid over the professor's fingers and curled up in his palm.

The professor smiled and brought this gunk up to his face.

With gentle fingers, he tried stretching the weird new substance. He rolled it into a ball and dropped it.

It bounced!

"Amazing!" the professor murmured. "Weebo! Take a picture!"

A flash unit rose from her oval body. "SMILE," she said.

Flash!

Startled, the green goo curled up into a blob and flung itself across the room. It ricocheted off the walls, the ceiling, the floor. Each time it bounced it made a deep, rubbery sucking sound, like a bathroom plunger.

Weebo spit out an instant picture just as the gunk bounced up the stairs—a picture of the professor and a green blur.

"It's amazing!" the professor crowed. "It's miraculous! It's—"

"GONE," Weebo noticed.

The professor and Weebo chased it upstairs.

Crash! The green blob escaped out a window

and bounced down the street.

Meanwhile, the professor frantically searched his living room closet. Oh, where was it . . . there! His old catcher's mitt!

The blob came bouncing back up the street. When the green gunk bounced back into the professor's house, Weebo ducked. But the professor reached out and caught it in his catcher's mitt as if it were a speeding baseball. He slapped his hand over the opening as the wad wiggled wildly, trying to get out.

"You know what we've got here?" the professor asked.

Weebo answered by displaying the complicated chemical formula for the green gunk. Then she said matter-of-factly, "FLYING RUBBER."

"Flying rubber?" the professor repeated. Then his face erupted into a huge grin. He held the stuff up and proudly announced the name of his new invention:

"Flubber!"

Weebo nodded her approval.

"But it's useless," he said, "if we can't control it."

Webber, the robot, followed as the professor hurried back to the basement. He put the Flubber in the tank and went back to work.

"The gamma rays will trigger the molecular reaction, which releases the energy that propels the Flubber . . . ," he mumbled.

At last—just as the sunrise began to peek into the lab—the professor seemed satisfied. He picked up a remote control and stepped back. "Keep your fingers crossed."

Weebo's screen popped up, showing two hands with fingers crossed.

The professor took a deep breath, then turned a dial.

The Flubber whimpered.

The professor turned the dial to the right.

The Flubber inside the mixing tank turned to the right.

The professor turned the dial to the left.

The Flubber turned to the left.

"It works!" the professor cried.

Beep-beep! rang an alarm. The professor glanced at his watch: 6:30. "The wedding!" he exclaimed. "It's starting. I have to go, Weebo."

Weebo flipped up her screen to display the time: 6:30 A.M.

"I'm aware of the time, Weebo," the professor said as he shrugged into his soiled tuxedo jacket.

Weebo displayed the day: SATURDAY.

The professor looked puzzled. "Your dates are wrong. I'm getting married on Friday at 6:30 P.M."

"YOU'RE NOT GETTING MARRIED— PERIOD," Weebo said. "YOU MISSED IT. IT IS NOW 6:30 IN THE *MORNING*."

The professor looked stunned. *"Oh, no! What have I done?"*

CHAPTER EIGHT

Saturday morning Professor Phillip Brainard raced across the quiet college campus as if he were late for class.

At the office of the president he quietly slid open the door and poked his head inside. Sara sat at her desk, working.

"Good evening," he said—hoping a little humor might help.

It didn't work. Sara didn't crack a smile. "You have a lot of nerve showing your face around here after what you did to me last night."

The professor stepped inside. "Can I explain what happened?"

"There's nothing to explain," Sara said firmly. "You weren't there. For the third time you left me standing at the altar."

"I apologize with all my heart. But listen, please," he begged. "*This* is why I didn't make it last night." He pulled a pulsing green ball out of his pocket. "Flubber!"

"Flubber?" Sara asked skeptically.

The professor explained as only he could. "It's a metastable compound whose molecular configuration is such that the delivery of minute particles of energy to its surface triggers a change in the configuration, which liberates enormous quantities of energy." He paused to take a breath. "Isn't that remarkable?"

"What's remarkable is that I ever fell in love with you," Sara wailed. "You broke my heart so you could stay home and make a ball of green goo?"

"Oh, but it's much more than that," he insisted. "Flubber can save the college! Let me demonstrate." He raced to the window and lugged it open. He stuffed the ball of Flubber in his back pocket, then climbed onto the windowsill. "When I hit the ground, the Flubber will send me right back up, unharmed. Watch."

"Are you nuts?" Sara cried. Her office was on the *second floor*!

The professor winked and backed out the window. "I'll be right back." Neither he nor Sara saw the ball of Flubber split the fabric of his pants and shoot out.

The professor dropped bottom-first to the ground.

Sara screamed and ran to the window.

But the professor—without the Flubber in his pocket—didn't bounce. When Sara looked out the window, she saw him sprawled on the ground.

"Ouch," he commented.

"If you're trying to get me with sympathy, you're wasting your time!" she shouted down at him. "We're *finished*!"

The professor winced as she slammed the window shut.

Last night's wedding had been his final exam with Sara.

He had a feeling he had just flunked.

CHAPTER NINE

Crunch!

"Ow!"

"Shhh!"

Smith and Wesson—Chester Hoenicker's security guys—crept through Professor Brainard's cluttered yard in the dark of night. They spotted him through the lighted basement windows.

The two men watched as the professor scooped up a spoonful of green powder, then stirred it into a jar of white face cream.

Next he dug through an old golf bag till he pulled out a golf ball. Then he smeared it with the "Flubber Cream."

Huh? Smith and Wesson exchanged a puzzled look.

Then the professor threw down a Flubberized golf ball. *Boom! Zing! Smash!* It bounced off the floor, ricocheted off the wall, and smashed through the basement window.

Clunk! Smith grabbed his head as he fell to the ground. The golf ball bounced off into the sky.

Wesson bent over his friend. "You okay? Man, that golf ball was *moving*! How'd he do that?"

Next the professor Flubberized a bowling ball—and bounced it.

Zoom! Wham! The bowling ball flew out the basement window, conked Wesson on the head, bounced off the driveway, and disappeared into the sky.

Down in the basement the professor smiled in satisfaction. "Flubber appears to have certain sporting applications."

Smith and Wesson staggered down the driveway, trying to get away, just as the golf ball returned to earth. And the bowling ball.

Bam! The men got bonked again, before the two balls bounced back into the sky.

Meanwhile, the professor poured some green liquid into a bottle with a spray nozzle. "Fluid Flubber—in the convenient spray applicator bottle," he said aloud. He tried squirting the spray out the window. *Psssssst!* The driveway sparkled green in the moonlight.

Outside, Smith and Wesson huddled against the wall, standing on trash cans. "When the bowling ball comes down again," Wesson said, "head for the car."

As soon as it bounced, the two guys jumped from the trashcans. Their feet slammed hard on the Flubberized driveway.

Boing! Smith and Wesson flew into the sky as if they'd bounced on a trampoline.

Crash! Smith and Wesson plunged from the sky. Howling, their faces black and blue, they hung like giant marionettes in the apple tree in the neighbor's yard.

Next door, the professor opened his garage door. He had a new idea about how to use the Flubber. But would it work?

About an hour later, covered with grease, the professor slid out from under his old 1962 Thunderbird convertible. "It's gonna work, Weebo." The professor had removed the engine and replaced it with a smaller version of the Flubber mixing tank.

The professor climbed into the car. "You want to go for a ride?"

Weebo zipped inside and hovered over the passenger seat.

"If it works," the professor said, "we'll fly over to Sara's house. If we park this baby on her roof, she might change her tune."

"MAYBE YOU SHOULD GO WITHOUT ME," Weebo suggested.

"Why?"

"I GET CAR SICK."

The professor shook his head. "It has nothing to do with cars. It's about Sara—and you'd better get over it."

He started the car and eased it out of the garage.

And then something miraculous happened. As it rolled down the driveway, it slowly began to rise in the air. "All right! We're flying!" the professor said. He pushed a button to lower the convertible top.

With a little practice, the professor began to

get the hang of driving a flying Flubber-fueled car. *Chirp-chirp-chirp!* He soared across the night sky, thousands of feet above the town. "Look at that, Weebo. All the world below and beyond. The stillness, the solitude . . ." He leaned forward and switched off the motor. "The silence." The chirping stopped.

Weebo spun around. Her screen filled with the face of a young woman in a horror movie— screaming!

And then the Thunderbird plunged toward the ground.

CHAPTER TEN

The professor hunched over the wheel, trying to start the motor.

Down, down they fell, through the clouds, until . . . a foot from the ground the motor clicked back on. The professor floored the pedal. And the Thunderbird streaked down the street.

Whew! The professor and Weebo took a moment to appreciate the fact that they were still alive. In a few moments the professor and Weebo were back in the sky and the Thunderbird flew toward Dr. Sara Jean Reynolds's house.

Dr. Sara Jean Reynolds and Wilson Croft sat on her front porch. She was trying to like him. Really, she was. But so far she just felt . . . irritated.

A shadow moved across the roof. It was the Thunderbird. Professor Brainard scowled as he hovered over them, listening.

43

"It's such a pleasure to spend an evening with you without Brainard hovering over us," Wilson said.

"I have to say good night," Sara replied politely. "I have a busy day tomorrow."

"I hate to see you work so hard for so little. You're trying to save a college that's sinking faster than—"

"I don't want to argue about colleges," Sara interrupted.

"Rutland College would die to have you," Wilson argued. "We'd be together with nothing but time."

It sounded good. To work at a college that didn't have money problems. And Wilson was a handsome, intelligent man. So why couldn't she stop thinking about the professor?

"Think about it—please," Wilson urged.

Sara sighed. "I will." She walked him down the sidewalk to his car. Wilson stopped and leaned forward to kiss her. . . .

Hovering above them in his Thunderbird, the professor's heart sank.

But at the last moment Sara turned her face.

The kiss landed on her cheek with a sloppy-sounding *smack*!

"I'm sorry, Wilson," Sara murmured.

"It's okay," he said, feeling foolish. "We have lots of time."

What am I doing? Sara wondered. Things would never work out with Phillip. Maybe she should give Wilson a chance. "I'll be driving up to Rutland for the basketball game Friday."

"I'll see you then," Wilson said.

"Should I make a dinner reservation for after the game?"

That gave Wilson an idea. "If Medfield wins, you buy me dinner. If Medfield loses, we go to the mountains for the weekend."

Up in the Thunderbird, the professor nearly exploded like an overheated test tube. But then he grinned and picked up an apple.

"Do we have a bet?" Wilson asked.

"Let me think about it." With a wave, she hurried inside.

Wilson pumped his fist in the air. "I can't lose. She's mine!"

Thunk!

45

An apple fell from the sky and knocked him to the ground.

On Weebo's screens, a baseball umpire shouted, "You're *out*!"

Professor Brainard pulled into his garage and slumped down in his fabulous new invention—a flying car fueled by Flubber. He should have been happy. He should have been thrilled!

But he was miserable. What did it all matter if Sara was lost to Wilson?

"I WISH I COULD MAKE YOU FEEL BETTER," Weebo said softly. "I WOULD NEVER TREAT YOU THE WAY SHE DOES."

"It's not Sara," the professor said. "This is my fault. I didn't show up at the wedding. I haven't done anything to help save the school. . . ."

"IF SHE LOVED YOU, SHE'D BE MORE UNDERSTANDING OF YOUR NATURE," Weebo said. "MAYBE I'M OLD-FASHIONED. MAYBE I NEED TO UPGRADE MY SOFTWARE. BUT I BELIEVE A WOMAN SHOULD LOVE A MAN FOR WHAT HE IS, NOT FOR WHAT SHE WANTS HIM TO BE."

The professor dragged himself out of the car. "This is a human matter," he said. "It's not for computers. It's for people." He sighed wistfully as he strolled out of the garage. "Good night, Weebo."

Two pairs of lips appeared on Weebo's screen. And they both sarcastically stuck out their tongues.

CHAPTER ELEVEN

Weebo waited until the professor had fallen asleep in his room. Then she flipped on the TV, careful to turn down the sound. She turned on a computer, too.

Weebo's red light flickered as she surfed through several channels. At last she saw what she was looking for.

A picture of a woman who looked something like Sara. Weebo captured her image with her camera lens. She changed the woman's eyes from blue to green. She changed her hair. She made her taller. Slimmer.

Then Weebo tried different clothing on the woman's image. Bathing suits, pajamas, jeans. At last she settled on a simple sleeveless linen dress and nice flat shoes.

A file on the computer opened, listing female names. Weebo selected Sylvia. Next Weebo positioned herself in front of the computer. A new file opened, and Weebo clicked on CREATE.

The computer's hard drive crackled. A powerful laser beam pooled in the center of the darkened room. Then slowly the image of a woman appeared. A hologram—a three-dimensional image as soft and fragile as a ghost. Sylvia.

The hologram of Sylvia opened her eyes, and Weebo sighed. If only she could make herself human, this is how she would be.

Sylvia walked upstairs to the professor's room with Weebo right behind her. He was still sleeping.

"PHILLIP?" Sylvia said with Weebo's voice. The image leaned over to kiss him.

Just then the professor's eyes snapped open.

He sat bolt upright in bed. "Weebo! I've got it!"

Sylvia disappeared in a puff of smoke. Weebo's screen slammed shut, and the lovesick computer fled down the stairs.

Weebo hurried to close her Sylvia file. She renamed it STORK. The computer's screen saver came on just as Weebo heard the professor on the stairs. "Weebo! This is brilliant!"

Quickly, Weebo turned around and backed

toward the wall to assume her bedtime position. An electrical plug popped out of her backside, and she plugged herself into the socket. She pretended to be asleep.

The professor ran into the living room. "Weebo?" He flipped on the lights.

Weebo slowly opened her screen.

The professor knelt beside her. "I've solved all our problems," he whispered excitedly. "Flubber's going to the basketball game!"

Weebo sighed. If only he could act that excited about her!

The next day the professor, Weebo, and Webber worked in the kitchen. Dozens of thumbtacks were stuck into the table as Webber sprayed them with paint.

"You're sure that the Flubber was fully fixed on the tacks before we painted?" the professor asked.

"POSITIVE," Weebo answered.

"And the wear-out time on the paint?" the professor asked.

"THIRTY MINUTES."

The professor nodded in approval. "If the Flubber worked right away, it'd look a little suspicious."

"DUH!" Weebo responded.

"It's crucial that we win the game," the professor said, pacing the kitchen floor. "I don't want to take any chances. I'm going to show Sara that Flubber works, and I'm going to do it right under Wilson Croft's nose!"

When the paint was dry, the professor gathered up all the thumb tacks and hurried out to his Thunderbird. Medfield College was playing Rutland College in basketball. With a little luck, he might just change history—and win back his girl.

As he backed down the driveway, the golf ball and bowling ball—still bouncing—just missed him as they hit the driveway and bounced back into the air.

The professor stopped by the kitchen window. "Make sure the Flubber stays in the tank," he called to Weebo.

Weebo's screens showed a little girl with a halo over her head.

The professor winked. "Thank you."

As soon as he drove off, the little girl turned into a little devil with horns and a mischievous grin.

CHAPTER TWELVE

In the Medfield locker room, Coach Willy Barker studied his starting players. They were clean-cut farm boys. And not a one of them was over six feet tall: Bart Bush, a skinny redheaded forward; Dale Jepner, a five-foot-seven center; Bruce Bagwell, a timid five-foot-two freshman guard; Werner Worley, a wiry forward; and Larry Romney, a stocky guard with glasses.

Coach Barker sighed. The game was about to start. It was time to give his team a pep talk. "Rutland has us in height, reach, weight, power, agility, skill, talent, offense, and defense."

This was depressing! The players hung their heads.

So no one noticed an equipment bag slide away from the bench.

Hidden behind the lockers, Professor Brainard opened the players' bags one by one and pulled out their basketball sneakers. Then he shoved a Flubberized thumbtack into each heel and toe.

"Rutland is undefeated in their last 108 games," Coach Barker added. "But that doesn't mean we can't whip these guys—right?"

The players stared at their coach. A few were close to tears.

Hoo-boy, the coach thought. Rutland's gonna cream us!

Professor Brainard crossed his fingers. The protective paint should wear off those tacks sometime in the first half—exposing the Flubber. But would it work?

Back in the professor's house Weebo and Webber had gone downstairs to the laboratory.

Yeah, yeah, the professor had told them to keep the Flubber in the tank. But what fun was that? WE'LL JUST TAKE IT OUT FOR A FEW MINUTES, Weebo thought. Who'd know the difference?

Webber opened the mixing tank. The Flubber oozed out. But when it saw Weebo, it whirred and slunk back inside.

Weebo whirred back.

Curious, the Flubber began to click.

Again Weebo copied the sounds—*click! click!*—then she made electronic sounds of her own.

Now the Flubber copied *her* sounds.

They were talking!

Flubber rolled back into a ball and whinnied in laughter.

Next Weebo snapped on her spotlight—*Flash!*

The Flubber went berserk! It bounced across the worktable, the floor, the ceiling, and up the stairs . . .

And then it was gone.

Weebo looked at Webber.

Ooops!

CHAPTER THIRTEEN

Weebo found the Flubber hiding in a cigar box and coaxed it out.

Now what? It was Friday night. How about a little dance party to celebrate the weekend?

Weebo's screen popped open, and she clicked on CD PLAYER.

Suddenly the room pulsed with Weebo's favorite mambo beat. Everybody dance!

The Flubber bounced, boogied, wiggled, and whirled. It broke into a dozen pieces and kicked up its feet in a chorus line.

Weebo rocked and spun around the living room as Webber did a clunky "funky chicken."

Then Weebo zipped into the kitchen and zapped the appliances.

Popcorn popped. The coffeemaker perked coffee to the beat. The blender whirled, and the dishwasher lights flashed like a disco while Webber did a shimmy with a dish towel.

Then the Flubber bounced onto the windowsill and split into two graceful dancers—like Ginger Rogers and Fred Astaire.

Behind them, the Christmas lights the professor never took down began to flash to the beat. Garden sprinklers shot up like exotic fountains, sparkling in the colored lights, till the Flubbery couple ended in a sweeping bow.

Then the lights all went out. Weebo, Webber, and the Flubber went to sleep. And the only sound was of the crickets chirping in the summer night.

Professor Brainard held his breath as the Medfield-Rutland game began. Rutland's seven-foot center grabbed the opening jump and headed for the net—slam dunk! First score Rutland!

The professor walked up the bleachers and sat down behind Sara and Wilson. Sara smiled politely, Wilson just sneered.

"I hope you're not a betting man, Wilson," the professor said.

Sara glanced sideways at Wilson. Phillip couldn't possibly know about their bet—could he?

"Go Medfield!" the professor shouted right in Wilson's ear.

The professor waited patiently, but the first half was painful to watch. The short guys on the Medfield team looked like middle school kids playing the Chicago Bulls. At halftime the score was—*Ouch!*—Rutland Rangers, 54; Medfield Squirrels, 3.

It was about time for the Flubberized tacks to go to work. But the professor decided a little extra Flubber couldn't hurt. He stood in the crowd by the locker room as the players headed back onto the court. He glanced around to make sure no one noticed. Then he opened his jar and scooped out a glob of Flubber cream.

"Let's give it to them this half!" he shouted, holding out his hands to the players.

Dale reluctantly shook the professor's hand.

Then the professor held out both hands. "Werner!"

Werner halfheartedly slapped him ten.

As Larry passed, the professor smacked him on the rear.

Each slap slathered extra Flubber on the players.

The professor hurried to his seat just after the second half had begun. He watched as the center threw the ball in for Rutland, and Bruce leaped and grabbed it on the fly. He passed to Werner. Werner dribbled downcourt and passed to Larry.

Blocked! Larry ran into someone and fell. *Boing!* His butt hit the floor, he bounced, and he sailed up to the net. *Swish!* The ball dropped through the net.

Rutland Rangers, 54; Medfield Squirrels, 5.

As the game continued, something miraculous happened: the Medfield Squirrels scored points!

A confused Rutland team spread out across their zone. Together they looked up in disbelief as the Squirrels bounced over the scoreboard.

Then Bruce leaped twenty feet into the air and dropped the ball! His teammate Bart flew into the air, caught the ball, and dunked. The score: Rutland, 66; Medfield, 50.

The Rutland bench players stared at the scoreboard in shock. The coach shot from the bench in a rage. "Are you blind?" he screamed at the referee. "They're doing something illegal!"

The referee shrugged. "Nowhere in the rule

book does it say anything about jumping too high!"

Medfield's score climbed to 54, to 59, to 63.

Fweeet! The referee called a foul, and Dale stepped up to the free-throw line for Medfield. He took aim. He shot.

The ball ricocheted off the backboard, shot to the opposite end of the court, hit the Rutland rim, and swooshed through Medfield's net.

Sara was cheering. Wilson was frowning. The professor pounded him on the head with a rolled-up program. "Did you see that?"

Rutland's ball. They pass. No good! Medfield's Dale stole it away! Passed to Larry. Larry shot the ball into the rafters! It dropped like a stone. . . . *Swish!* Unbelievable!

Rutland, 66; Medfield; 67. The Rutland coach called a time-out.

Beaming, Medfield's Coach Barker gathered his boys at the bench. He was so excited he could hardly speak. "Fourteen seconds to go," he told them. "Just do what you're doing—whatever the heck it is!—and don't let them score!"

The players nodded.

But Dale was looking at the bottom of his shoe. That's odd, he thought. Somehow he'd stepped on a couple of tacks.

He didn't know they were *Flubberized* tacks. He didn't know that *they* were the reason Medfield was about to win the first game in the history of the school.

Up in the stands Professor Brainard slowly rose to his feet. "No," he whispered. "No, Dale. *No!*"

Dale yanked out the tacks and tossed them under the bench.

Professor Brainard sank to the hard seat and moaned. He watched as Larry saw Dale, then checked his own shoes and removed the tacks. Down the bench, like a tumbling row of dominoes, each player looked at his shoes and pulled out the tacks.

Fweeet! The referee called the players back to the game. Rutland's ball. The Medfield players glued themselves to their opponents as they moved down the court.

With a confident grin, Dale jumped . . . a foot. Dale stared down at his feet as if they'd betrayed him. Then he watched someone from Rutland fly above him and stuff the ball through the net.

The score: Rutland, 68; Medfield 67.

Time left on the clock: 00:04.2 seconds.

The Medfield fans groaned.

They'd almost tasted victory. There was no way could they win now.

"Wow. What a bang."

The Professor and Weebo share breakfast.

The Professor explains Newton's theory of gravitation—to a confused group of art students.

He remembered his tuxedo—if only he could remember to attend his wedding.

The absentminded professor at work on his newest creation.

Not all of the Professor's inventions work out so smoothly.

Flubber's birthplace.

Flubber makes a face.

Webber dims the lights and swings to the mambo.

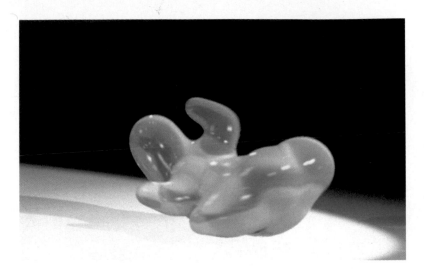

Flubber gets down on the dance floor.

With the Professor's newest invention, Medfield may actually win their game!

With a little Flubberized mechanics, the Professor's vintage T-bird will soar to new heights.

The perfect housemate!

In a twist on tradition, the minister tells Sara, "You may now kiss the video screen."

CHAPTER FOURTEEN

"This is an emergency!" The professor shoved through the crowd. "Excuse me, I'm an educator. Excuse me. . . ."

At last he reached the bench, where Coach Barker was in shock. "What happened?" he gasped to his players.

The professor tapped the dazed man on the shoulder. "I don't know much about basketball, Coach. But I do know chemistry, and I'd say the problem your center's having is in his shoes. Do you have any alcohol?"

"What?!"

"Never mind, I have some. I'll just clean the bottom of their shoes."

"Are you crazy?!" the coach exclaimed.

"Nope. Absentminded maybe, but not crazy." The professor quickly knelt down. "Hello, Dale. Let me see the bottom of your shoe."

Puzzled, Dale lifted his foot as the professor slipped the Flubber fluid from his pocket. "You're playing great," he said.

"*Was,*" Dale said glumly. "It'll be on my shoulders forever. We were on the verge of winning our first game ever, and I blew it."

"It's not over yet," the professor reminded him. "Keep your chin up." He emptied the bottle of Flubber on a towel and swabbed the bottom of Dale's shoes. Then he looked the boy square in the eyes. "When you get the ball, jump with all your soul."

Dale shook his head. "With less than five seconds, I won't get very far."

"You did it before, you can do it again," the professor insisted. "As soon as you get the ball—jump!"

"But I'll be on this end!" Dale complained.

Professor Brainard was desperate—he used the only weapon he could think of: "You get the ball and jump, or I'll *flunk* you!"

The whistle blew and the players moved back onto the court.

Dale was nervous. He glanced at his coach,

then up at the professor waving at him from the stands. He tried a little hop. *Boing!* Hey! He was bouncing again! He waved, and the professor shot him a thumbs-up sign.

Down on the court the ref gave the ball to Medfield's Werner, then stepped back and blew his whistle.

Werner was nervous, his hands sweaty. He spun the ball. It glistened with Flubber.

Rutland's center leaned over Dale, blocking him completely.

Werner was in a panic. There was no one to pass to!

The professor leaped to his feet. "Jump, Dale! Jump!"

Quickly Dale leaped thirty feet into the air and grabbed the ball with only a second to go.

Dale touched down at half-court and bounced again! He tucked into a roll, flipped toward the basket, straightened out . . . and dived headfirst through the net!

Ennnhhhhh! The buzzer sounded. The game was over.

Rutland Rangers, 68; Medfield Squirrels, 70.

The gym exploded in shouts and cheers.

"We won! We won!" the professor whooped. Without thinking, he grabbed Sara and whirled her around. Then he realized what he was doing and let go. "Uh, congratulations, Sara."

But Wilson was furious. "Since when is it within the rules for a player to accompany the ball through the net?"

"Come on, Grumpy," Sara teased. "I owe you dinner." Then she took Wilson's arm and left the stadium.

The professor's joy over the victory popped like a balloon. How could she still go out with that creep?

"I don't know how," Wilson griped as he walked Sara to his car. "But I'm absolutely *certain* your team cheated."

Sara laughed. "You're just being a sore loser."

Just then the professor caught up with them.

Wilson groaned.

"Can I talk to you for a moment—alone?" he asked Sara.

"What you have to say to her, you can say to

both of us," Wilson snapped. "If you can *remember* what you were going to say."

The professor glared at him but turned to Sara.

"Flubber?" he said hopefully. "Ring a bell?"

"Flubber?" Wilson sneered. "Sounds like baby shampoo."

The professor just ignored him. "Sara! Flubber won the game."

Sara frowned suspiciously. "What do you mean?"

"The shoes!" the professor exclaimed. "I Flubberized the shoes. That's why the players could jump so high. And I put it on their hands so they—"

"Are you serious?" Sara demanded angrily. "You're taking credit for Medfield beating Rutland?"

"I'm not interested in credit," the professor insisted, laying his hands on her shoulders. "I'm simply saying that tonight you saw, firsthand, Flubber at work. It's remarkable, isn't it?"

Sara shoved his hands from her shoulders. "*You're* remarkable."

"But I'm telling you the truth!"

But Sara wouldn't listen. She slid into the car and slammed the door.

"What do we have to do to get you to take a hint?" Wilson growled. "It's over—you lost. Go home and play with your Flubber."

The professor watched them drive off into the night.

His Flubber had helped Medfield win the game. But when it came to matters of the heart, Phillip Brainard was still a loser.

CHAPTER FIFTEEN

When the professor got home, Weebo was waiting for him by the screen door.

"WHO WON?" she asked.

"We did," the professor said sadly as he came in the door.

"WHY THE LONG FACE?"

The professor took a bottle of water out of the refrigerator and sat down at the kitchen table. "Bad night."

"CARE TO ELABORATE?"

"I think you know."

Her screen slowly rose, showing a picture of Sara.

The professor took a sip of water and sat back in his chair. "If I understood human beings, if I understood women, if I understood emotions. If I understood any of that, I wouldn't have spent my life in a laboratory trying to figure out how the world works. I would have been out in the world trying to figure out *why* it works."

Weebo's eyelike screen was filled with a live picture of the professor talking. Without telling him, she was videotaping everything he was saying.

"I know I love her, Weebo. The neurons in my limbic system are saturated with phenylethylamine, which causes feelings of elation, exhilaration, and euphoria. The truth is, Weebo, I'm not absentminded because I'm crazy or inconsiderate or selfish. I'm absentminded because I'm in love with Sara.

"I don't have any more chances with her, and that's probably just as well. It's over. She has to move on. I'm not right for her. You're the one for me, Weebo. I know you're not fond of her. You didn't want me to marry her. I guess, in a way, you were right. So I'm all yours. It's just the two of us. And the Flubber makes three. No more Sara."

He stood up and headed for the stairs. "Good night, Weebo. Sleep tight." He turned off the lights and headed up the stairs, tired and defeated.

Weebo hovered in the entry hall. Her screen rose slowly, and a scene from an old movie played so only she could hear.

"I'm so in love with him," the actress in the movie was saying, "that I want him to have what he wants—even if it means you instead of me."

Alone in the darkness, Weebo hovered in front of Dr. Sara Jean Reynolds's house. It would be so easy just to leave things as they were. Sara would be out of the picture, and Weebo would have the professor all to herself.

But he'd be miserable. And how could Weebo be happy with that?

With a sigh, she sailed up to the second-floor bedroom window. "SARA," she called softly. "I'M SORRY TO WAKE YOU, BUT IT'S IMPORTANT."

Sara bolted up in bed, startled, but then hurried to the window. "What's wrong? Is everything okay with Phillip?" She opened the screen so Weebo could float inside.

"PHILLIP WOULD BE VERY ANGRY IF HE KNEW I LEFT. HE'D ALSO BE ANGRY THAT I WOKE YOU UP. BUT I HAVE TO SHOW YOU SOMETHING. DO YOU HAVE A MINUTE?"

Sara nodded, and Weebo flipped open her screen. The professor's sad face appeared. Then Weebo played the video she'd just made at the kitchen table:

"I know I love her. . . . The neurons in my limbic system are saturated with phenylethylamine, which causes feelings of elation, exhilaration, and euphoria."

Sara couldn't help but grin at the professor's own special way of explaining love.

"The truth is, Weebo, I'm not absentminded because I'm crazy or inconsiderate or selfish," she heard him say. "I'm absentminded because I'm in love with Sara."

Sara's heart melted.

Weebo's electronic equivalent of a heart twisted in pain.

CHAPTER SIXTEEN

After watching Weebo's video, Sara rushed over to Phillip's house and awakened him with a kiss. He tried to explain to her about Flubber—then decided to show her.

Now she clung to the dashboard, terrified, as Phillip's Flubberized Thunderbird whooshed them into the night sky.

Grinning, the professor parked near a bank of clouds, with a good view of the moon. "So, what do you think?"

Sara didn't move. She didn't speak.

"Sara?" the professor asked worriedly.

Suddenly she turned to him, her eyes glowing. "This is it! This is the solution. *This* is how we can save the school!"

"That's what I've been saying," the professor responded. "Flubber. You saw what it did at the game. Imagine the line of shoes we could develop."

"Not shoes, Phillip," Sara said impatiently. "This! *Flight!*"

Together, gazing at the moon, they made plans.

An hour or two later, the Thunderbird touched down in the driveway, and the professor backed it into the garage.

The headlights went out. The garage door closed.

Suddenly the overhead lights flipped on.

Chester Hoenicker smiled down at them like a shark, flanked by Smith and Wesson. Bennett stood nearby. "It's a pleasure to finally meet you. I believe you know my son, Bennett. He *used* to play basketball for Medfield."

Bennett smirked at the professor.

The professor took Sara's hand as they slid out of the car.

"Lovely old car," Mr. Hoenicker said. "There's a lot of money in your . . . what do you call it? Flubber? Perhaps we could make a deal—"

"Flubber belongs to Medfield College," the professor said.

"At the end of the term there isn't going to be

74

a Medfield College," Mr. Hoenicker snapped. "I'll forget the debt you owe me right now if—"

"No, thank you," Sara cut in.

"The Flubber is not for sale," the professor agreed.

"When I leave," Mr. Hoenicker said, "I take my offer with me."

"I understand," Sara said.

Mr. Hoenicker shook his head. "Good luck," he said sarcastically. Then he and his men strode out of the garage toward a black Mercedes.

Whomp!

The bowling ball and the golf ball got Smith and Wesson one more time.

CHAPTER SEVENTEEN

A few days later Mr. Selden, a very busy executive at a car company sat at his desk going over some paperwork.

Honk! Honk! Honk!

His assistant hurried to the window and threw open the shades.

Selden glanced up from his work—and his jaw dropped.

A 1962 Thunderbird was parked just outside the window—and this was the tenth floor!

The professor waved. Sara held up a sign that read FOR SALE.

Selden shoved his other work off the desk. He had a very important meeting to hold with the owner of that car!

The lights were out at the professor's house. The Flubber purred contentedly in its tank in the basement. Weebo and Webber were watching the home shopping channel on the living room TV.

But Weebo's screen kept drifting closed. Soon she was asleep.

Suddenly—*Crash!*—Smith and Wesson kicked in the kitchen door.

Weebo's screen flashed open with pictures of cymbals. Webber's arms flashed out in panic. Downstairs the Flubber stopped purring.

The men's flashlights crisscrossed through the darkness as they hurried downstairs. Tables overturned and test tubes crashed as they searched in the dark for the professor's green stuff.

Eeeek! The Flubber shrieked as Smith's flashlight beam fell on the mixing tank. "I think I found it," Smith chortled.

Thunk! Weebo crashed into Wesson's head, knocking him down. She zoomed around again and—*Pow!*—Smith hit the floor. Terrified, the men huddled in the darkness trying to figure what had hit them!

Weebo switched on her spotlight and scanned the room.

But that just made *her* easier to see.

Wesson grabbed a baseball bat lying on the floor. And the next time Weebo zoomed past—*Wham!* he clobbered the little computer.

Weebo bounced off the wall, then crashed into the trash can.

Wesson held up the bat and peeked inside.

Weebo was dented and scratched, and her camera lens was shattered. Worst of all, her center seam was split. Battery fluid oozed from the gash.

Across the room the Flubber wailed.

The moon sparkled on the ocean as the professor and Sara soared home. What a great meeting they'd had with Mr. Selden!

Sara held up their check. A check with a *lot* of zeros. "I never thought I'd see a check for five million dollars." She slipped it into her purse. "Are you sure you can make more Flubber? You remember the formula?"

"Me?" The professor shrugged. "I forgot it thirty seconds after I made it."

Sara gasped. "B-but—"

"It's okay." The professor chuckled. "It's on the computer."

Whew! Sara thought. Thank heaven it was safe.

Safe? Uh-uh. At that very moment Professor Brainard's computer was parked on a desk in Chester Hoenicker's library. Nearby, the terrified Flubber trembled in its tank.

Smith and Wesson had stolen both from the professor's house.

And Mr. Hoenicker had his own professor to work on the Flubber.

The professor and Sara stared through the busted kitchen doorway in horror as Webber automatically swept up shards of glass.

The professor raced down the stairs to the basement. The Flubber—it was gone! "Weebo!" he cried out.

When he found the little computer in the trash, his heart froze.

She wasn't moving.

Carefully he picked her up and cradled her in his arms. "Weebo? Can you hear me?"

A single file name flickered on her screen. STORK.

The professor tenderly stroked her polished black surface. "I'm going to take you upstairs and get you on AC and download you onto . . ."

Weebo stopped whirring.

"Weebo!" the professor shouted, trying to call her back.

The file name STORK faded from the screen.

And even the brilliant professor could do nothing to save her.

Weebo was gone.

CHAPTER EIGHTEEN

The Thunderbird blasted out of the garage and into the sky.

The professor reached into his pocket and pulled something out.

"Phillip!" Sara cried. "Not a gun!"

"It's just a squirt gun," he assured her.

"Wouldn't it be better to just call the police?" she asked.

"And tell them what? They wouldn't understand Weebo. To them, she'd just be a machine, and I'd be some insane scientist." The professor shook his head. "I have to deal with this myself."

"*We* have to deal with it," Sara said gently.

The professor smiled. Then he reached into his pocket again. "Load the gun."

He handed her a bottle of Fluid Flubber.

"I had a feeling you two eggheads might drop by," Wesson said as he opened the door at

Chester Hoenicker's mansion.

Moments later Sara and the professor sat down in Mr. Hoenicker's living room—with Flubberized thumbtacks stuck in their shoes.

"I'm prepared to sell you the Flubber," the professor announced.

Smith and Wesson snorted with laughter. They'd just *stolen* the big blob of green icky goo. It was in the library down the hall!

"You been to your house recently?" Mr. Hoenicker asked with a sneer.

The professor's anger grew as he thought of what these thugs had done to Weebo. But he just nodded. "Flubber's hard to control. Have you tried to do anything with it?"

Mr. Hoenicker shrugged. "I've got my own scientist working on it—"

"I can make it easier for you. Give us a thirty-day extension on the loan," the professor bargained, "I'll tell you everything you need to know. I'll make as much Flubber as you want."

Mr. Hoenicker's eyes glittered. "I'll tell you what. I'll give you the thirty days. And you give me two years. Whatever you come up with over the next two years is mine."

"That's not fair!" Sara protested.

Hoenicker shrugged. "Shop somewhere else, lady."

"It's all right, Sara," the professor said. "I'll do it."

As they walked to the library, the professor secretly clicked the Thunderbird's remote control. The car rose into the air and followed them above the house. Then, with all its lights turned off, it hovered just outside the French doors.

"You're going to enjoy this," Mr. Hoenicker said. He led them into the library, where a man sat with his back to them, working at Phillip's computer. "Professor!" Mr. Hoenicker called to the man. "I brought you a little help."

The man stood and turned around.

Sara gasped.

The man grinned at Sara and the professor. "The lovebirds," he said sarcastically. "Welcome."

It was Wilson Croft!

CHAPTER NINETEEN

"Finally quit teaching?" the professor quipped, trying to mask his fury. He shouldn't be surprised—a creep working for creeps.

Wilson shrugged. "How could I pass up an opportunity to transform the energy industry?" He stepped out from behind the desk. "Flubber is very interesting, Phil. Too bad it's so unstable. I was just looking over the formula. Dangerous mix."

"There's a way to deal with it," the professor said. He crossed to the mixing tank and reached into his pocket.

Wesson grabbed his arm. "Hey!"

The professor smiled and held up a small jar. "Hand cream," he fibbed. "So the Flubber won't stick." He rubbed some on, then tossed the jar to Sara. "She has to help me."

When the professor reached into his other

pocket, Wesson grabbed his arm and checked the pocket himself. He took out the gun.

The professor chuckled. "It's a squirt gun. To lower the temperature of the Flubber," he fibbed again.

Wilson nodded, and Wesson handed back the gun.

Then the professor twisted open the tank. Everyone took a nervous step back.

"It's okay," the professor cooed to the Flubber. "It's me."

Wilson rolled his eyes.

"Shhhh!" the professor said as he reached into the tank and pulled the Flubber out. "Everybody be still." Then he went and stood by the window, the Flubber in the palm of one hand. His other hand felt in his pocket for the remote control.

He glanced at Sara. She nodded slightly—she was ready.

"Do it for Weebo," the professor whispered to the Flubber.

The green goo whirred.

The professor jabbed the remote. The Thunderbird's landing lights flashed through the

French doors, blinding them all.

The Flubber squealed and took off.

Smith and Wesson drew back their fists to punch the professor. But he jumped in his Flubberized shoes and bounced above their heads.

And Smith and Wesson punched each other in the face.

Wilson grabbed for Sara. But she pummeled him like a punching bag with her Flubber-creamed fists, and he sank to his knees.

Bennett picked up a large glass paperweight.

The professor whipped out his gun and quickly squirted the back of his pants with Fluid Flubber.

Then, just as Bennett threw the paperweight, the professor turned and stuck out his rear end.

Boing! The paperweight bounced off his butt and bonked Bennett on the head, knocking him out cold.

Meanwhile, Sara jumped into the air and caught the bouncing ball of Flubber. The professor caught her as she came down. She offered him the Flubber, but he shook his head. "Go ahead."

Sara grinned and wound up her arm like a

major league baseball player. "This one's for Weebo." She threw it as hard as she could toward Mr. Hoenicker, who was trying to escape.

Thwack! It smacked him in the back of the head and—*Crash!*—sent him smashing through a large glass window into the bushes below.

Wilson stared, his mouth wide open, as the Flubber zoomed back across the library—and right into his open mouth.

He gagged, clutching his throat. Then his chest. Then his stomach and guts. The Flubber whirred as it raced through Wilson's entire digestive system.

Suddenly Wilson clutched his stomach. He grimaced as a loud explosive *Riiiiiip!* filled the room.

The freed Flubber bounded out of the library.

Wilson looked over his shoulder in horror. There was a huge hole in the seat of his pants.

His last thought before he fainted was he wished he'd never heard of Flubber!

The professor brushed off his hands, then smiled at Sara and held open the French doors to the garden. "After you."

Boing! She and the professor jumped into the front seat of the hovering Thunderbird, then headed home.

Below them the Flubber bounced down the street, across town, over the backyard fence, and into the professor's bedroom.

It landed in the catcher's mitt—*thunk!*—with a loud sigh.

Home at last!

CHAPTER TWENTY

Later that night the professor and Sara sat on the front porch. They had beaten Chester Hoenicker and made enough money to save the college. But their victory couldn't erase the pain of losing Weebo.

The professor searched the constellations in the summer night sky, as if they might hold the answer. "What happens to the soul of a machine?"

"Can you fix her?" Sara asked softly.

He shrugged sadly. "I can make repairs, but I can't bring back whatever life it was that she had. That's gone. I don't know where it came from. I've tried to find it. I've tried to recreate it."

Suddenly Sara remembered something. "What was that word on her screen at the very end?"

"I don't know," the professor answered. "She was damaged. She could have displayed anything."

"Do you remember what the word was?" she pressed.

The professor shook his head.

"Try." Sara grabbed him and kissed him. "Do you remember now?"

Hmmm, it was coming back to him. "It began with an *S*."

She kissed him again, harder.

"It was a bird."

She kissed him so hard it knocked him over.

"Stork," the professor whispered.

Moments later they typed "stork" into the professor's computer. The folder opened, showing several files. One read: DEAR PHILLIP.

The professor was afraid to open it, so Sara took the mouse and clicked on the file.

They gasped at the image of a beautiful woman smiling back at them from the screen. She spoke in Weebo's voice. "Hello, Phillip. It's me. Weebo. If I were human, that is. If you're reading this, I'm no longer here. I don't know what happened to me. But I hope my demise did not cause you any undue stress."

She paused for a moment, then confessed, "I

never wanted you to reproduce me, because I couldn't stand the thought of having to share you with anyone else. It was a very selfish thing to do.

"Sara? I'm sorry that my jealousy got in the way of us getting to know each other better."

Sara nodded, though she knew Weebo could no longer see.

"Phillip? A full and complete design of me is in this file. You didn't forget it—I never showed it to you. I've made some changes, removed a few of my flaws—and added a little of you."

There was a long pause.

"I hope you can love my daughter as much as I loved you," she said softly. Then she blew him a kiss goodbye.

As the professor returned the kiss, his eyes filled with tears.

And then Weebo vanished forever.

CHAPTER TWENTY-ONE

Bells rang out from the Presbyterian Church on Beech Street. Organ music filled the air. The church was packed with people.

Sara Jean Reynolds waited for her wedding to begin. As she walked down the aisle, she knew what some people were whispering.

The professor wasn't there—*again*!

But this time Sara didn't care. She knew how he felt, and she knew where he was. In fact, she could see him right now.

At the altar she smiled at Weebo's red daughter, Weebette. She could see the professor— live—on the flying computer's twin screens. He was all dressed up, tinkering on his latest experiment in his basement lab. He smiled happily and waved.

The minister began. "Wilt thou, Sara, take this man to be thy wedded husband. . . ."

Sara smiled as the minister repeated the age-old words, then answered emphatically, "I will!"

The minister smiled in delight—and relief. "For as much as these two people have *finally* consented together in holy wedlock, and pledged their troth by giving and receiving rings . . . sort of. And by joining hands . . . sort of . . . I pronounce—believe it or not!—that they be husband and wife. Amen, and hallelujah!"

The minister smiled at Sara. "You may now kiss the screen."

The professor puckered up. *Smack!* Sara left a big red lipstick mark on Weebette's glass screens, then they walked down the aisle.

"I'll meet you at the reception," the professor promised. "I'm almost done. This is going to be remarkable."

"Please be careful, Phillip," Sara whispered, a little worried.

The professor winked, then stepped back from the camera and poured two chemicals into a single beaker. "These two chemicals are completely compatible. There's absolutely no chance of—"

Blam! The screen went fuzzy.

Sara winced. He'd probably blown up the lab again.

Oh, well! Life with the professor would never be boring!

A 1962 Thunderbird chugged through the sky with a sign reading JUST MARRIED scrawled across the back.

The professor honked, and Sara waved at a passing plane.

Then Mr. and Mrs. Phillip Brainard soared off through the clouds in their Flubberized Thunderbird to begin their new life together.

It was going to be a crazy ride!